DEMAIN I

CW00809266

Short Sharp Shocks!

Anthologies

The Darkest Battlefield – Tales Of WW1/Horror

FANGED DANDELION

POEMS BY
ERIC LAROCCA

A BEATS! BALLADS! BLANK VERSE! BOOK

BOOK 5

For further information, please visit:
WEB: www.demainpublishing.com
TWITTER: @DemainPubUk
FACEBOOK: Demain Publishing
INSTAGRAM: demainpublishing
Dave Dick: https://www.davedickillustration.com

CONTENTS

ACKNOWLEDGEMENTS

There are countless people to whom I'm forever indebted. Without their assurance and dedication, I am certain that *Fanged Dandelion* would not exist.

I wrote much of this collection while the United States went into lockdown due to the Covid-19 pandemic. Admittedly, I never imagined any of these poems would see the light of day simply because they were so deeply private and revealing. In fact, none of these poems would have been finished if it weren't for the gentle comfort and encouragement of my partner, Ali. He shepherded me through some very tumultuous times when my outlook on life was bleak at best. I cannot thank him enough for all the affection and warmth he's shown me. I only hope I can return the favor one day.

Next, my heartfelt gratitude belongs to Dean M. Drinkel of DEMAIN PUBLISHING. Our professional relationship began thanks to a chance encounter on social media. I had tweeted that I was searching for a small press to partner with in order to publish a small poetry collection and Dean kindly reached out, expressing he would be interested in taking a look at the manuscript. Within a day or so, he sent me an email welcoming me and my work to the DEMAIN PUBLISHING family. Dean has been an absolute delight to work with and I couldn't be happier to have found a home for my work at DEMAIN.

I would be remiss if I didn't take this opportunity to sincerely thank Sara Tantlinger for sacrificing so much of her time to craft such a beautifully written Foreword for this collection. I have been a dedicated fan of her work for quite some time and it feels so surreal to have her name associated with this book simply because I adore her writing so much.

I am also very thankful for the talent and devotion of artist Dave Dick who has illustrated the interior artwork for this paperback version of *Fanged Dandelion*.

Finally, I would like to take this opportunity to dedicate this book to anybody who feels as though they're weighted down with grief or burdened by trauma. I urge you to take comfort in the fact you are not alone. Be gentle to yourself and set yourself free.

Eric LaRocca

FOREWORD

Eric LaRocca has already established himself as a fresh and exciting voice within horror prose, so imagine my excitement when I learned he writes poetry, as well. LaRocca's debut poetry collection, *Fanged Dandelion,* is a short work that ensures every poem, every line, and every word bite deep into the reader's veins.

Always curious about the history of a thing, I did some research and discovered that 'dandelion' derives from a 14th century French term: *dent-de-lioun,* 'lion's tooth' in reference to the jagged leaves. The origin fits this collection so flawlessly for within there are teeth and a lion's hunger, a desire to slice open a human and see what makes them tick, to plunge fangs into a lover's heart and consume their bleeding passion raw. However, there are also phrases as gorgeous and delicate as a flower's gentle petal—it is within this balance where LaRocca truly shines. His ability to show us something beautiful and also all the ways it will make us scream is, for me, what makes perfect horror poetry.

Clever and poignant, each poem plays with ideas in unexpected ways, and I found that every time I reread a piece, I discovered a new way to imagine or interpret what could be happening within those twisted lines. The format of the titles, such as 'venom in bløøm' and 'no lōnger human' shows unusual choices, allowing the reader to pause and think about what the poem could have in store. Those moments of savoring each title in a unique way before diving in adds a whole new layer to the collection, and LaRocca never disappoints with his delivery.

Dandelions are such cheerful plants with their bright yellow flower, inviting a wanderer to pluck its stem from the earth. They have a long history of being used as food, as herbs within medicine, and more, so to reimagine the dandelion as something seeping in shadows was an enjoyable experience throughout the book. Nature's beauty offers rich splendor and a chance to connect with the earth, but there also exist things within nature that are truly strange and terrifying. Within *Fanged Dandelion,* LaRocca captures both points of view—the beauty and the eccentricity, the light and the alluring darkness. It is an impressive feat to be able to do that so well in only twenty poems.

Inventive imagery shows itself in lines such as "I'd leak my brain / until it was the size / of a dressmaker's thimble / burn the bad thoughts / until they screech..." where we are treated to a lyrical cadence that holds nothing back. Also images like, "candied viscera / luscious, succulent / too decadent to eat / a saccharine trelliswork / where bones disagree..." stayed in my mind long after reading the words. Every depiction is so richly painted, and each poem deserves to be slowly tasted in the reader's mouth.

The fantastical splendor of darkness where lush language seeps from the imagination of shadows holds the reader captive. Lines like "I knit a dreamcatcher / from bloodstained ivory / a glittering puzzle / buried beneath an / exquisite red plant..." invite us into a nightmare garden where we're never really sure what may be lurking beneath the crimson leaves and serrated foliage, but it is such a pleasure to discover all the twists and turns along the way. Passion and fear intertwine in pieces like 'lovesick arms' and 'brainsick xo' where we are not quite sure what a lover's hands or teeth may be capable of, but it's such a sick joy to read along and find out.

Within this garden of flesh and teeth, LaRocca invites the reader to drown in the lush imagery, but there's also a chance to see our own darkness reflected back at us. In LaRocca's introduction to *Fanged Dandelion,* he beautifully explains one of the greatest fears of all—a fear of ourselves, of our own brains, of what we might be capable of doing during these times of unexpected emotional and mental chaos. Poetry can be especially cathartic because it allows the writer to be vulnerable in short bursts where every word matters—there is no time for fluff or filler, which LaRocca knows because every word within is a beat of the heart's poem. It's needed and necessary, even when it's painful.

Horror holds such an important place in the hearts of us who have felt that fear, who have felt marginalized or othered in any way because it forces us to look in the mirror and ask if we are the fanged dandelions smiling back at society. Maybe we are, but LaRocca shows us the petals, the beauty, the alluring glisten of bleeding our pain onto the page and having it come together to create something entirely our own. A work that could only ever be created by someone who understands what it means to evaluate the light and the dark hovering beneath their own skin.

One of the things that makes LaRocca's writing so compelling is his truth, his ability to take life and have it reflected on the page in striking, unexpected ways. It has been a treat to read (and reread) this collection. I truly cannot wait to see what the future has in store for Eric LaRocca's talented, lyrical, and wickedly delightful work.

<u>Sara Tantlinger</u>
Bram Stoker Award-winning author of *The Devil's Dreamland: Poetry Inspired by H.H. Holmes*

INTRODUCTION

I had never been frightened of myself before.

Of course, fear had claimed me at a young age when I found myself lost at an amusement park at the age of five.

I'm still forever indebted to the park ranger who reunited me with my parents not long after I realized I was lost.

In fact, as I now reflect on my formative years, I realize fear played an instrumental role in my upbringing. I was afraid of anything and everything.

Whether it was imagining catastrophe awaiting me on the bus during the morning commute to school thanks to a reckless driver or pondering the many ways in which my parents could meet an untimely demise while I was separated from them, I was an expert in the subject of fear. Caution preceded every play date with a new friend, trepidation was present at every event with crowds of people.

I lived in a permanently nervous state for much of my childhood. I thought I had imagined practically every horrible scenario of what could happen to me and my loved ones.

Imagine my surprise at the age of twenty-six when I considered myself to be the cause of catastrophe. Imagine the depth of my horror when I contemplated how easy it might be to swerve into oncoming traffic or to plow over an unsuspecting herd of pedestrians. I had been afraid of everything and anything. But I had never imagined myself to be capable of doing something truly horrible.

It was perhaps the most frightening moment of my life—wondering if I really knew myself, if I could possibly conceive of executing such gruesome tasks. I don't take any pleasure in reliving these thoughts, especially my brief excursion to the emergency room because I was so overwhelmed with the intrusiveness of each thought.

Thankfully, I was able to confer with highly regarded doctors in New England and later became medicated.

In March of 2020, humanity capsized, and fear spread its fingers across the face of the world as the coronavirus pandemic surged. As civilians retreated to the comfort of their homes, I found myself isolated in my brand-new apartment in Cambridge, MA and noticed familiar (and unwelcome) thoughts spiraling in the corners of my mind. Although I was comforted by my boyfriend, I felt powerless once more and worried about the moment when my pernicious thoughts would turn to him.

So, as a last-ditch effort to thwart any possibility of entertaining thoughts related to harm falling upon my loved one, I began writing. As difficult as it was, I sat down at the keyboard and began working on a new project. I found myself writing short verses (almost stream of conscious-type material) as opposed to the methodically planned prose I had come to practice over the years.

I was surprised at myself—I had never considered writing poetry before and yet I found myself compelled to venture further into unknown territory as two words arrived at the front of my mind: Fanged Dandelion.

As perplexing as the term first appeared, I considered its presence further and wondered if it might be some shorthand to describe the mechanics of my brain. After all, how could my mind—an organ that facilitates the creation of countless literary works of art—turn against me and render me a basket of nerves? My parents had always praised the ingenuity of my mind ever since I was small. Why is it that my mind turns against me?

It was then I considered the term 'fanged dandelion' and thought of it as an embodiment of my mind—something ornate and delicate yet filled with the possibility of peril.

Writing this collection of poems was deeply cathartic for me.

I found myself exploring topics I thought I would never acknowledge on paper. I gave myself permission to be vulnerable and I was able to write about things I had been too apprehensive to previously explore—ideas of self-perception, family, identity.

In many ways, I was able to be even more honest with the reader by exploring these concepts in a poetic form as opposed to a traditional fiction narrative. Although I still adore the mechanics of fictional storytelling, I was completely enraptured with the process of writing poetry and really appreciated the level of honesty the format afforded me.

While I didn't necessarily purge these intrusive thoughts, that was never my intention when writing this collection. I'm able to live comfortably now with many of these thoughts operating below a whisper.

If you're reading this and you happen to find your mind blossoming with a similar fanged dandelion, remember there are far more petals than there are fangs.

1. ABOMINATION TO A DAISY [PROLOGUE]

If a beetle
is an abomination
to a daisy,
my mind has
four skittering
black legs and
my body is a
windswept summer field

2. FANGED DANDELION

I am a vile thing
made of insect hair
and broken teeth
a wrinkled mouth like
a wasp's nest
he kisses me "goodbye"
anyway
stings him just a little
the briar planted
in my tongue
a fanged dandelion
wrapped
in hemlock and
wormwood
petals of my skin
peel like decoupage
a music box my mother
had made me
for when I first
returned home
a "thank you" for not
hurting her again
or perhaps a bribe to
keep away from her
something hisses
inside an eggshell

my father cracks
on the frying pan
asks me "what are
you doing here?"
calls me names
like "monster"
an oily corpse spills
out into the dish
I take a bite
imagining it's him

3. XXX_CANDIED VISCERA_XXX [INTERLUDE]

I sew
my shadow
to his breath
peel his skin
off until he
glistens
like a broken
shard of moonlight
I pour honey
into the hole
I've opened
candied viscera
luscious, succulent
too decadent to eat
a saccharine trelliswork
where bones disagree
joints grinning
seams ooze amber
buttons burst syrup
"it's been so long
since I've tasted you"
I gorge until I'm full
sweating his blood

4. VENOM IN BLØØM

as we dream
drowsing in starless sleep,
I watch his ghost feed
on me, drinking
nectar from the rotted
slice of fruit
broiling inside my skull
I see his jaw stretch
open the way a snake's
does, lips vacuuming
me like a black
balloon being pulled

over my head
he smears the dew
across my face
with the bone from
his mouth, something
quivering inside me
like a small insect
trapped
inside the tomb of
a carnivorous plant
he'd drink it all if he could,
turn as sickeningly green
as seawater
his mouth
a tourniquet
for venom in bloom
"there, my love,"
he says
his jaw shrinking
like an elastic band
an ivory maggot
withering
away in velveteen sunlight
"no more bad thoughts"
unwrapping
himself from me
and suckling from damp
threads of moonlight
I sprout from beneath my skin

as if it were a paper cocoon
I perch myself
upon the bedpost
needle-thin fingers
rooting through
the brawn of my brain
the same way a primate
grooms another
searching for
something he had missed
something horrible
and torn
by its stem only to
be replanted
in the dark soil
where I know
his tongue can
never find

5. HIS GRINNING SPINE

chrysanthemum kiss
my vertebrae smiles
lips slit in half
rotted tongues pruning
I unwrap a ribbon of
scarlet from his throat
he thanks me for
being so tender
I prop his arm with
pins and wires
just like I had done
with the small bird
I had found on my
walk this morning
wings speared with
little toothpicks
a voice whispering,
"I'm not ready to let you go yet"

6. ONCE THE ROOTS HAVE A TASTE [INTERLUDE]

boiled mouths sprout
red weeds I was once
too scared to water
and me, without my pail
what would make you stay?

7. THINGS CAN'T GET MUCH WORSE

coppery taste
when my eyes open
as if I had been
sucking on a penny
my hands bound with
wire and duct tape
a cottonmouth still has
fangs when it's asleep
mother reads downstairs
father cooks in the kitchen
slicing a carrot
snip
snip
his finger
ouch
I loathe myself for
entertaining the thought
I want to be the one
holding the knife

8. THE_BONE_WEAVER

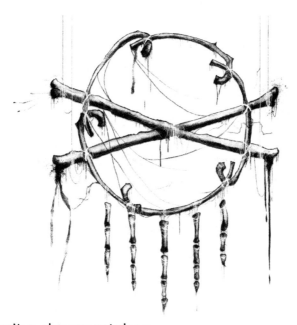

I knit a dreamcatcher
from bloodstained ivory
a glittering puzzle
buried beneath an
exquisite red plant
I had never seen before
I hang the shattered bits like
hard candy beside my bed
and hold a funeral for him
and the seeds I had planted
in his breath that were
never to bud

9. LOVESICK ARMS

I might snap him like
kindling if my hands
would let me
feast on the grizzle
flowering where his
spine bends in
frightened prayer
he asks me when
I'm coming home
to him
"when I'm better," I say
he knows that won't
be anytime soon
"your parents can't
take care of you the
way I can," he tells me
but I haven't told him
how much it hurts
me to be around him
to think the things
I do about him
to imagine him
without eyes
without arms or legs
to gleefully feed on him as if
he were a speck of grain

and I were nothing
more than a mealworm

10. I BUILD COFFINS [INTERLUDE]

I build coffins
from needle-thin
slivers I pluck from
my spine as if they
were growling quills
I bury loved ones
in tansy and lace
until they're choked
like the gravesides
of sick children
who had died with
red faces and swollen lungs

11. A MOTHER IS A KIND OF GOD

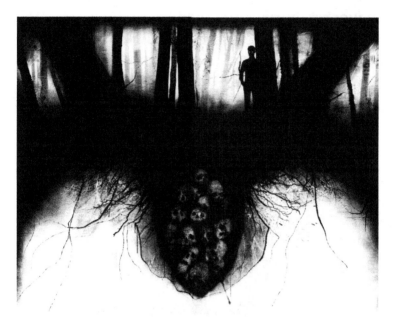

Sometimes I dream you call me "mother"
My children are delivered into coffins
when they're born
their bloodless corpses as tiny
and as shriveled as white
maggots deserted in sunlight.
Gloved hands scrape them
from the warmth of my bowels
and do little to interrupt
the blood leaking like molten
lava from where their little

bodies have been hastily ripped away
Sometimes as
many as three at a time are found –
the remnants of
makeshift burial sites hidden away
in my darkest recesses.
"He seems to prefer you,"
a man in a uniform says to me
regarding my children's father –
a fugitive that only ever
seems to visit me after twilight.
"He doesn't bring them
anywhere else." And why should he?
After all, he knows full well no
other companion would scarcely
take care of his offences with such devotion.
Like clockwork, he calls upon me
when daylight's been vacuumed away –
a slim man in tattered flannel and dark
overalls, toting a canvas bag and a small
toolkit.
Digging me open with a small
spade until a new hole
yawns back at him, he delivers
another child and plants
her deep inside me – a knifed
brunette curled inside a large rucksack.
He promises me he didn't rape her,
and I show him

gratitude for little mercies such as that.
I'm tender with her as she spills into
me, my roots clutching her bruised
body as if telling her I'll be the only
mother she'll ever need.
Of course, it's little comfort for the agony
she's already endured, but I
promise her that the worst is behind
her and she seems to soften as if grateful
He helps her burrow
deeper inside me because some of
the other ones have been
uprooted before they were ready,
nighttime predators clawing
through my entrails until I'm numb
and dragging my dead children
off to their dens to be devoured.
"Not this time," he says to me,
closing me up until any evidence
on my body of his presence has been erased.
"You promise to keep this one
hidden for a while?" he asks, almost
pleading with me as if he's a
servant to my fancy and not
the other way around.
I think of all the others I've
protected for him
the auburn-headed girl from
Providence he had met at the local

movie theatre and had asked if he
could give her a ride home only to bash her
over the head with a crowbar.
I remember how she was still alive
when he had first buried her
inside me and how our heartbeats had
tethered to one another
before hers finally dimmed, swallowed by a
bed of my dirt and gravel.
I think of the dark-haired girl he had
met in Boston and how she had
begged him to stop even after
she had told him she was pregnant.
I recall the weight of her body
the lifeless cargo hardening like cement
inside her – and how deep
they both sank after he had pushed
them inside me.
He leaves me and I'm finally
left alone with my new precious bundle
my womb cradling her gently
as if it were a useless apology
for her father's brutishness
I command little insects to
consume the fear-scented dew from her skin
cleaning her body the way a mother
deer cares for her fawn.
It's the least I can do for her
Then, I demand tiny buds to

sprout and grow a bed of lilies from
where she's been planted –
the grave he's made of me.
It won't be long before others
will come searching for her
combing through the hemlock
and pines where my hair grows or
scouring the mushroom-filled
glen where my legs meet
They'll pluck her out of me,
flowers slashed and left desecrated
until he eventually returns
again with another body for me to hide
another unloved child for the
majesty of my forest to bear

12. NO LŌNGER HUMÄN

black flies circling
eyelids sliced with
livid paper cuts
I find him curled
inside a tree trunk
sprouting red metal
lapping rainwater
from a branch that
resembles a limb
he used to have
dreaming of when
he was once human
when his bones were
like handmade cradles
before I had defiled him
worshipped his disgrace
like an orphan without eyes

13. HANDLE WITH CARE

skin melting like ice
in a drink I couldn't finish
quarantine for two weeks
she's tender with me
as if I'm marked
"fragile handle with care"
all mothers are like that
stovetop hums alive
chamomile scent
to calm my nerves
little flame blooms
I push her hand toward it

want to see her hands swallowed
burned until fingers turn black
skin fumes
crackled like patent leather
it's my way of thanking her
for giving me things like
the teeth of the moon
something I never asked for

14. BRAINSICK XO

skull smashed with a hammer
little bugs scurry through cracks
I drink from there as well
ladle the thoughts creeping
around the way small crabs do
pinch the fear rooted in
the awkward goodbyes
"please don't leave me"
he begs when we're undressed
bleeds out like a wounded deer
when I peel the rust from
beneath his fingernails
the only thoughts I'll eat from him
I haven't fed in days

15. TOOTHLEŠŠ [INTERLUDE]

winter's virgin martyr
a crucified tongue
whispers obscenities
to me and promises
to protect me from
the glass splinter rotting
inside my toothless smile
dangling from my mouth
for all to see
like a jeweled fishing lure

16. NIGHT TIDE

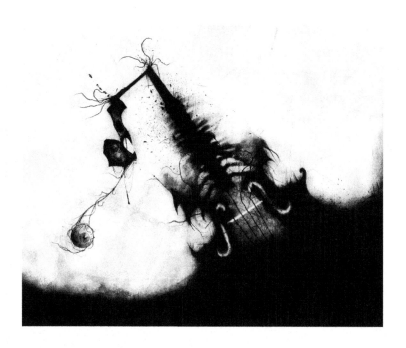

soul crusted black
like the burned carcass
of an insect that once
tried to devour me
while I was sleeping
I dreamed of stabbing
him in the eye and then
plucking his veins as if
they were violin strings
"why do you think
about hurting the ones

you love so much?"
stones in my pockets
to keep my body down
as the night tide drowns
the reeds I had planted
gurgling when I say
"because if I didn't
someone else would"

17. THIMBLE

cannibal priests
with their collars
as sharp as the
tips of ladies'
fingernails refuse to
baptize me
because I've already
eaten the
thoughts they bury
in charnel pits
lovingly interred
mercies left unsaid
the atrocities done
to innocent children
temporary hosts
for their pleasure
stretchy skin shrivels
like sunbaked fruit
I keep one eye closed
to resemble
the kind of creature
they call me
"you're a monster
for even thinking it"
and perhaps they are right
I'd leak my brain

until it was the size
of a dressmaker's thimble
burn the bad thoughts
until they screech
like starving children
having their
fingernails ripped off

18. SOMEONE ELSE'S SKIN

saintly centipede
a smile like a steel trap
I'm going to die wearing
someone else's skin
I'd crawl out of the hole
in my face if I could
parasitic mouth, something
for him to chew on
while he decides if he
still loves me or not
I don't bother to wait

I nail myself to a tree
and hang there like a
bag of spoiled fruit
hair whitens, teeth chip apart
like fine china

19. IF IT BLEEDS [INTERLUDE]

I need help, someone
please do something
I would have never
cut a hole so deep
in my abdomen if
I had known how
much it would hurt

20. CRAWLSPACE [EPILOGUE]

I tuck him deep
inside the crawlspace
in my mind
feed him little morsels
like crickets and worms
I wonder if he'll do
the same for me
when I can no longer move
when I'm his prey

BIOGRAPHY

Eric LaRocca's fiction has appeared in various literary journals and anthologies published in the US and abroad. His debut novella, *Starving Ghosts in Every Thread*, was released in May 2020.

Please visit him on Twitter: @ejlarocca or visit ericlarocca.com for more information.

ADRIAN BALDWIN (COVER ARTIST)

Adrian is a Mancunian now living and working in Wales. Back in the 1990s, he wrote for various TV shows/personalities: Smith & Jones, Clive Anderson, Brian Conley, Paul McKenna, Hale & Pace, Rory Bremner (and a few others). Wooo, get him! Since then, he has written three screenplays—one of which received generous financial backing from the Film Agency for Wales. Then along came the global recession which kicked the UK Film industry in the nuts. What a bummer! Not to be outdone, he turned to novel writing—which had always been his real dream—and, in particular, a genre he feels is often overlooked; a genre he has always been a fan of: Dark Comedy (sometimes referred to as Horror's weird cousin). *Barnacle Brat* (a dark comedy for grown-ups), his first novel won Indie Novel of the Year 2016 award; his second novel *Stanley Mccloud Must Die!* (more dark comedy for grown-ups) published in 2016 and his third: *The Snowman And The Scarecrow* (another dark comedy for grown-ups) published in 2018. Adrian Baldwin has also written and published a number of dark comedy short stories. He designs book covers too—not just for his own books but for a growing number of publishers. For more information on the award-winning author, check out:

https://adrianbaldwin.info/

DEMAIN PUBLISHING

To keep up to-date on all news DEMAIN (including future submission calls and releases) you can follow us in a number of ways:

BLOG:
www.demainpublishingblog.weebly.com

TWITTER:
@DemainPubUk

FACEBOOK PAGE:
Demain Publishing

INSTAGRAM:
Demainpublishing

Printed in Great Britain
by Amazon